NO ONE
WANTS TO
LIVE HERE

NO ONE
WANTS TO
LIVE HERE

MARK HOLDEN

NEW MICHIGAN PRESS

TUCSON, ARIZONA

NEW MICHIGAN PRESS

DEPT OF ENGLISH, P. O. BOX 210067

UNIVERSITY OF ARIZONA

TUCSON, AZ 85721-0067

<http://newmichiganpress.com/nmp>

Orders and queries to nmp@thediagram.com.

ISBN 978-1-934832-45-5. FIRST PRINTING.

Printed in the United States of America.

Design by Ander Monson.

Cover photograph by Sue Lezon.

CONTENTS

THE NEW BABY

THE MOTHER HAD BEEN HOME for five days. She didn't
know if she liked being home or not, but that's how
it had worked out. She was in the kitchen when her
husband woke up. He came in in his pajamas and said
he'd make the coffee. He asked her how she was.

She said she was fine. She showed him how fine by
stretching her lips across her teeth. She felt as if she
were four years old and posing to have her picture taken
so everyone could see later how happy she had been.
She said the baby was asleep. The husband went in to
see it, then came back and made coffee. *She's still sleeping,*
he said. The mother nodded. She didn't want to overdo
it. When the coffee was done the husband poured them
each a cup. She made him a piece of toast. He ate his
toast and drank coffee. Then he got up and left the
kitchen to get dressed. He came back a few minutes later.

He poured himself a second cup to go, kissed his wife, and then he left for work.

Five minutes later the mother threw their new baby out the window. It rolled like a sled through fresh snow, over a four-foot span of shingles beneath their second-story dormer window, directly above the first floor tenants' living room. Sometimes, as she and her husband sat in their own living room, they could hear the downstairs couple's TV, or hear the man belch after dinner during Wheel of Fortune. He had colitis, he'd told them, and he'd recently had a colonoscopy that went bad. He didn't say how bad it went, but now he belched loudly and explosively for about fifteen minutes after he ate. Sometimes they could hear his wife, too, say something to him in a soft voice after he belched. They couldn't hear what she said. They wondered how bad it went.

The baby rolled off the roof, its pink blanket unfurling. It didn't make any noise, then disappeared from the mother's sight. It dropped twelve feet and landed in the snow. The mother listened for a moment, but she didn't hear it hit the ground or cry, and then she closed the window. She looked over at the next-door neighbor's house, where Mrs. Pulchaski lived, and who often peered out from her kitchen window. The mother thought she might have seen her head—like a dried, spiky thistle top—pass behind the glass, but then it was gone.

No wonder the man downstairs had colitis. He and his wife filled up a big plastic garbage bag with Diet Pepsi cans in about two weeks' time. They left the bag on their tiny porch entryway. They put it next to a bag of rock salt and a shovel. She didn't know what they did with the cans—whether they recycled or threw them out, but every two weeks, after the cans grew on top of each other and morphed into one thing in their filmy cocoon, they disappeared like a moth in the night, and then it started again.

She wondered if Mrs. Pulchaski had seen her throw the baby out. She didn't really care if she did or not. The mother knew the people downstairs were gone; she'd heard them pull out for work this morning, before her husband, as they routinely did. The woman's car had a hole in the muffler. The woman worked as a bank teller, and the man as a car mechanic, but he'd said they didn't have the money to fix the muffler now. His wife was overweight, with skin like brown mustard, with purple rings under her eyes and a large upper lip that hung down over the lower one like a horse or a moose. The mother couldn't tell what she was—maybe a mulatto, if that's what they were called, if you could say that, or if it made sense, which the mother wasn't sure of. Now that America had a black president who called himself a mutt, maybe it didn't matter. Nowadays, no one knew what anyone was. *You couldn't tell a nigger from a lamppost. You couldn't tell one from the president.*

The mother surprised herself to think that. She would never *say* that to anyone, not in a million years. But no one was around, thinking was private, and a million years was up. The n-word formed itself, by itself, and hung behind her eyes like an old sign on a new store flipped from *Closed* to *Open*....

The woman's husband, though, was as white as the Irish and had a dragon tattoo on his back—a big scaly green one with red wings flapping across his shoulder blades—and the mother had seen him on more than one occasion in the summer, showing off shirtless, while he tinkered with their cars in the parking lot.

He hadn't liked it when she'd said the dragon looked like Champy, Lake Champlain's local version of the Loch Ness monster.

On Sundays, she knew he covered up the dragon and went with his wife to the First Assembly of God church, and at Christmas and Easter they took the woman's younger brother with them, then brought him back to their place for a holiday treat, for a turkey dinner which the mother and her husband could smell cooking. The odor of drumsticks and gravy came up through a gap between the pipes where they passed through the floor to the sink.

Except for those two days, the woman's brother lived in a special home for the disabled. The mother didn't know if you could say *disabled* or *retarded*. She only knew you were supposed to pretend that crazy people

were normal, even if their flies were unzipped or they
were running down the street with dead fish.

One Christmas, she happened to bump into them
as they were getting out from their car. She said *Hi,
how are you?* to the boy, who she'd learned had Down
syndrome. He had Down syndrome and some other
things wrong with him, but she didn't know what
those other things were. Sometimes he yelped, and the
mother wondered if he yelped in church. He looked up
at her as his sister helped him out of the back seat. She
held his arm as if to guide him. She said, *He's sixteen,
but he can't talk,* and the mother said, *That's all right,*
and then she jumped out of the way when the boy, like
a monkey, tried to grab her. He yelped when his sister
yanked him back.

He likes you, is what his sister had said, and the
mother acted as if it were perfectly normal for him to
like what he liked, even if he couldn't have it, even if he
never could.

AS FAR AS THE MOTHER KNEW, there was nothing
wrong with her new baby, but it clung and sucked like
a leech she'd once gotten between her legs. It was a
demanding, sucky, drooly thing she could barely stand
to hold or even look at; it cried and burped in her face
and shat in her lap. Its little fingers latched onto the soft
tissue of her breasts like the pincers of some insect. It
had the belly of a tick and the mouth of a lamprey eel.

She wondered who would come to the door first: her husband, a neighbor, or the cops. Whoever it might be, she'd be ready. She went to the back bedroom where, when they'd first moved in, they'd tried to remove the stinking, moldy plaster behind the fake wood paneling. When her husband went to remove a panel, the wall began to crumble. Then he pushed the paneling back and nailed it in place, and that was the end of their home improvements. Now she reached back into the closet where it smelled like mice for his Remington pump-action shotgun and the box of shells he kept on the floor, behind a pair of shoes.

In the kitchen, she made herself a coffee and loaded the shotgun the way she'd seen her husband do it. She pushed five shells into the magazine. She pumped one into the barrel. She flicked off the safety, put the gun on the floor, drank a coffee, and crossed her legs.

No one came. She sat and sipped her coffee and then got up to make a toast with jam. A half hour passed. It was eleven o'clock in the morning. She wondered what had happened to the baby. She went outside to look.

It wasn't snowing, but it had the night before, and now the blowing wind and snow stung her cheeks. It blew from the northeast and took her breath away. She slipped on the driveway's packed snow and ice. She walked over below the window where it must have fallen and found a depression, a hollow spot like an empty bowl, with tracks around it. The unfurled blanket, caught on something, flapped from the gutter.

She looked at the hollow spot and then she looked up the street. There, a dog was tearing into something like a bag of groceries. Shredded parts of it broke away and some of what was inside flew out. The dog picked up a piece and threw it playfully, like a stick or a bone, into the air and over its head. *Good*, she thought.

She headed back inside against the cold when Mrs. Pulchaski came out her own back door. She wore a coat over a bathrobe and rubber boots that went up to just below her knees. She looked over at the mother and said, *I saw what you did.*

So? the mother said.

So I saved her.

The mother looked up the street. She saw the dog worrying a loaf of bread.

And the cops will be here in two minutes, Mrs. Pulchaski said. *I'm going to tell them what you did, and maybe they'll give the baby to that nice young couple that lives below you. What do you think of that?*

Where is it? the mother said.

Suddenly Mrs. Pulchaski looked less sure of herself. Mr. Pulchaski wasn't home.

She's safe inside my house, she said.

The mother walked to the outside stairs of their back entrance that looked more like a fire escape—but which they preferred and always used because the front door brought you directly out into the street, making you feel naked and vulnerable. Mrs. Pulchaski watched her go and felt the blustery, frigid air against her cheeks;

then she went back inside too. The baby was asleep. Mrs. Pulchaski had gone out earlier and scooped it up out of the snow, checked to see if anything was broken, and when she found that nothing had been, placed it in a blanket in a cardboard box, then dug out the things she'd kept for when her grandchildren came to visit: things like baby bottles and rattles and extra diapers and toys. She washed one of the bottles, put a nipple on it, and warmed up some milk and gave it to the baby.

The cops hadn't come before the mother went back for the shotgun and over to Mrs. Pulchaski's. She let herself in through the back door, into the kitchen where the two of them were, and shot Mrs. Pulchaski, who'd been quite surprised to see the mother and that small, perfect circle of the barrel. Just before her face disintegrated from the buckshot and reformed itself into a majestic red pancake on the wall. That quick. Mrs. Pulchaski's blood sprayed the baby in the box. It didn't seem to mind the blood or the noise, or the second blast, which blew the head off its mother, who had turned the shotgun on herself.

The cops were still there, surrounding the Pulchaskis' house with yellow tape, when the husband came home for lunch. An ambulance idled in the road, and a crowd of onlookers mingled on the sidewalk. A few began to walk away, some of them openly weeping.

The husband knew his wife wasn't in the best of spirits, so he'd stopped at the drug store for a box of Russell Stover chocolate turtles, one of her favorite things. She liked them better than the cherry-filled. She liked them better than Whitman's. They were in a heart-shaped box with a picture on top of the kind of chocolates you get when you open it up. The picture made the chocolates seem bigger and better than they really were.

Judging from the commotion next door, it was obvious something tragic had happened—it wasn't just the cops helping the EMTs put someone in an ambulance—there was all that tape, bright and fluttering above the snow like banners at a used car lot.

His first thought was that one of the Pulchaskis had hurt the other. Last year, at their daughter's wedding reception, Mr. Pulchaski had sprayed his wife with a high-pressure water hose and made her dress go up over her head, which made everybody laugh. Another time he'd stabbed a watermelon with a screwdriver, pretending it was his sister-in-law who, he'd once told the husband, visited too often, cheated at nickel-dime poker, and drank too much of his good liquor. From the driveway, looking up at Mrs. Pulchaski, who was looking out through the kitchen window, he'd stabbed the watermelon and said *See? See? This is Blanch. Can't she buy nothing?* Then he kicked it like a football and hurt himself, claiming it was his wife's fault—*All of it, everything, goddamn it,* he'd said.

Those were the first two incidents that came to the husband's mind. He pulled into his driveway and waved to one of the cops coming out the back door of the

Pulchaskis' with a cardboard box. The cop couldn't wave back because his hands were full. Then he paused and looked left and right, as if he didn't know what to do next. The husband thought it seemed like he wanted to ask him something.

The husband felt sorry for the Pulchaskis and the cops. He stepped out of the car as a German shepherd ran down the street with a plastic bag of bread in its mouth. *People and dogs*, he thought. *What a circus*. He almost laughed. Then he saw the pink blanket hanging from the gutter.

The cop, having decided, put his box in the front seat of a cruiser. When he set it down, the baby started to cry. Another cop was sitting in the driver's seat. He seemed to be waiting for the day to end. Now he tried to rock the box. He couldn't really rock it, so he wiggled and shook it the best he could. She hadn't cried the entire time they'd been in the house, not even when they'd picked her up to see if she was all right, to see if the blood was her own, but now she started. The man in the driveway looked over.

The cop who'd put her in the car stood outside it and leaned on the open door. He tapped snow off the tops of his shoes and, having decided something else, after saying something to the cop behind the wheel, closed the door and looked back at the man in the driveway. Then he put on his hat as if he meant it, with both hands.

The husband had heard the baby. He thought the cries had come from the cruiser, but maybe they hadn't. He couldn't hear them now. The wind was swirling—it must have fooled him; probably his wife had opened a window for some air and the cries had come from above.

The cop approached. The husband wanted to go up the stairs to the apartment. He would invite him up and they could talk there. He would ask the cop if that would be all right. He would tell him he was worried. Then they could go up and he could check on things and they could talk in the kitchen, and he'd tell him what he knew about the Pulchaskis, about the hose and the watermelon.

He would give his wife the chocolates. He was sure she would open them right up and, before taking one herself, ask if anyone else would like one. She'd hold the box out to the cop first, as if he were a guest, and then she'd make an offering to her husband. He'd tell her about the blanket, how a gust of wind must have sucked it out the window—when she'd opened it, when she wasn't looking, when she was paying more attention to the baby—and then he'd ask her how she couldn't have known that it was gone.

STORMTRACKER 6000

TINA KESSLER CLIMAXED during "Weather *Plus*." She
didn't know what *plus* meant, exactly, as she had just
moved upstate from Cobleskill to Trout River, New
York, and if you could believe the claim below the
giant apple painted on the barn, it was home to the
largest McIntosh orchard in the world. But now she
wasn't driving past the apple, she was in her favorite
chair—and this was her first local TV weather forecast.
It excited her, this not knowing what the *plus* meant.
And Stormtracker 6000—what was that? Tina slipped
off her panties. She touched herself and imagined
a Humvee—that's what Stormtracker must be: a
customized weather vehicle with mounted cameras,
driven by young, lanky muscled men in their twenties…

Her legs hung over the chair's armrest, the chair
itself turned sideways to the TV, her toes pointed at
the weatherman, Roman Buchholz. She didn't know

if she liked him. He wasn't very handsome, but you couldn't be choosy if you wanted to come in the middle of the six o'clock news. You'd better be ready to take what you could get. You'd better be ready for guys like Roman. But instead of imagining him in her fantasy, she imagined three young men, three *storm trackers*, who lifted her dress up over her head, who peeled off her stockings and panties and carried her naked to bed. They asked what they could do for her. Tina told them what to do. She made them do it. Then she came in the face of Roman Buchholz.

Tina slumped back in her chair as Roman clicked his remote control, which changed the weather map to a five-day forecast. The forecast chart was full of clouds and raindrops. He said he was sorry, it didn't look so good. He was sorry for the people who were going to take a vacation in this shit—he didn't say *shit*—but you could tell that's what he wanted to say, what he really meant. It was July, he knew everyone wanted it to be sunny, but there was really nothing he could do. Then he said the weekend was looking better. He clicked his little box again, and two more days appeared: Weather *Plus*. So that's what it meant—five days *plus* two days. They stretched the limits of everyone's imagination. They stretched the weather out with graphic clouds and raindrops, more days, and a sun with yellow rays which appeared under *Saturday* and *Sunday*. Roman said that was good news.

Okay, Weather *plus*. But Stormtracker 6000? Tina righted herself in the chair and slipped her panties back on. They were the tiger striped ones she'd bought at Victoria's Secret. No one had seen them on her yet, so they were still secret. She thought she looked good in orange-yellow and black. She liked the way they made her feel. She imagined that someone, somewhere, would enjoy skinning the tiger. She wiped her wet fingers on the arm of her chair. *You wish, Roman,* she said.

Over the next few days, she learned more about weather and the other meteorologists. Channel Six had four of them on rotating schedules. She hadn't realized until now how demanding the weather could be. It was more demanding, apparently, than the news itself. Channel Six usually had two people report that. They were members of a team, like co-captains. No, they weren't co-captains, they were *anchors*, that's what you called them. And these co-anchors seemed like nice people. Tina thought she might have seen the man, Harold Langland, on a bicycle, pedaling along Lakeshore Road in black tights and a plastic blue helmet. The helmet came to a point at the back of Harold's head. She'd surely seen the woman, Nakeesha Davis, buying All-Bran and bananas at the grocery store. You couldn't mistake her for someone else. An antelope. A swan. A black leopard. Nakeesha was all of those. Tina wondered how Harold kept his composure. Maybe they gave him a Xanax before the news. They were so nice, these two people, like hair stylists or realtors. After a while you just wanted to kill them.

ONE THING TINA SORT OF DISLIKED about Roman Buchholz was the way he wore his jacket: the sleeves hung down past the wrists; they drooped to the back of his knuckles. Still, all of the weathermen, when they got serious, took off their jackets and rolled up their shirt sleeves. *Bring it on*, they seemed to say. Even Roman Buchholz wasn't such a girly-man when a real storm was brewing. *Let me show you what's going on*, he would say, with some authority. Or, *This is the situation…* He puffed out his chest when he said *mixed bag*.

Later, Tina was disappointed to learn that Stormtracker 6000 was not a Humvee, but a weather radar satellite. They called it part of the *Eagle Eye Radar Network*. The *Network* was all of the stuff combined: the computers, monitors, and satellite. At least that's what it seemed like. But the Stormtracker's map and colorful graphics were what people could actually see. When Michael Pipzinski, one of the other meteorologists, pointed to the map, he showed you things like red blobs and white lines moving across a green world. The world was basically green, according to Mike, and the weather moving across it was red and yellow, and sometimes purple. Occasionally he pointed to Lake Champlain, which was blue, and told you how high the waves were, or that the water temperature was *doing a dipsy-doo*. Maybe he'd say that someone had spotted Champy, the

lake's monster, in Cumberland Head bay. *Ha-ha.* Or
Mike would pan back on the map so you could see what
was happening in Albany, as if anyone cared about that.

Tina thought Mike Pip was all right. His jacket
sleeves draped nicely at the wrists.

Tina liked coming during the weather forecast,
whether it was reported by Roman, Mike, or one of the
others. She liked coming with her legs arched over the
cushioned arm rest, her vagina rising up in their faces.
She'd come home and slip out of her work clothes:
sneakers, t-shirt, jeans or shorts. She'd listen to the
news, play with herself, and imagine cumulus clouds
and storm trackers.

Tina could seldom escape the smell of the food she'd
served at the Snow Goose Diner where she worked: of
burgers or fish, or french fries. Sometimes she smelled
like men—what they ate and what they carried. That
was the worst, really—the old timers with their boiled
dinners or Michigans, those hot dogs with chili and
onions, mustard and hot sauce. She tried to leave the
men behind, but they came home with her as grease or
stale smoke. They couldn't smoke in the diner, but they
carried it in on their jackets and in their hair and gave
it to her. They were mostly farmers and prison guards
with baseball caps and big trucks, bad hearts and false
teeth, and their wretchedness, along with their bacon,
followed her home and into her living room, where, with
her hand between her legs, she melted in her chair.

She almost always came at six-fifteen. That was

fifteen minutes after the main news, after local politics and tragedies. She came once after hearing Nakeesha Davis say that a young man, Albert Lemieux, had shaken a baby girl. The baby was alive, but just barely. Now it was in a coma. Albert was not the baby's father, who, Nakeesha said, had recently moved to Alaska. Here in Trout River, the mother had gone shopping for wet wipes, and left Albert with the baby. She'd trusted him, she said, but realized afterwards that that had been a mistake. Nakeesha reported that Mr. Lemieux said he hadn't meant to shake it. He was only trying to wake the baby up, to show her the replay of Eli Manning's touchdown pass to Mario Manningham. He said he was pretty sure she liked football; he knew she liked warm beer. *Manning to Manningham!* he'd told her. *Manning to Manningham!* But she wouldn't wake up.

No one seemed to know if the baby would live or not. Nakeesha said everyone was hoping that it would. She looked sadly at Harold, who nodded solemnly. You could tell that he was trying to hope. It was hard to tell what he was hoping for though, because Nakeesha wore a low-cut blouse, and her microphone, clipped beside the top button, was pulling it off, tugging at it like a tiny black beetle. You could see cleavage. You could see freckles and lace. *Holy shit*, Tina thought. *On the local news?* She wondered how Harold could stand it.

Another time, Tina gave herself a powerful orgasm when they talked about bass. Nakeesha and Harold said the bass tournaments had begun. Everyone was having fun, Nakeesha said, catching largemouths and smallmouths. They caught them on top with hula poppers and jitterbugs; they caught them deep with plastic worms. Then Harold said the fisherman came from as far away as El Paso, Texas, to fish in Lake Champlain. They rented rooms, bought gas for their boats, and drove around in their trucks, pulling their trailers and stopping in restaurants to eat. Harold said that was good for the economy. He seemed happy to say it.

But one local man, who had been interviewed by a Channel Six reporter at the Snow Goose, said he didn't like the tournaments. His name was Al Skillings. He'd sat at the counter and poured four sugars in his coffee. Tina remembered serving him. He'd wanted pecan pie, but they were out of that, so she convinced him to settle for apple. Now, on TV, he said that the bass were dying. *Fishing isn't supposed to be like that,* he said. *Not the way they do it, poking their fingers in the gills, sloshing them around in plastic bags at weigh-in. Like a goldfish…Ever buy a gold fish in a bag, Missy?*

At the diner, the reporter Stacy Miller thanked him for his opinion. Then they edited out everything after *not the way they do it.* After she'd talked to Al, she told the cameraman to focus on the mayor. The mayor, whom they interviewed for the bass segment as well, was having bacon and eggs at a table with some friends, or maybe members of the Common Council. *The bass don't die* he'd said. *They catch them and let them go. Why do you think they strike?* he laughed. *They know they're going back.* Tina remembered how the mayor looked around the table to see who was laughing and who was not.

She thought the mayor had looked thinner in person, at the restaurant; on TV, he looked pudgy. Now Harold looked at Nakeesha after reporting what the mayor had said. They didn't seem to know if bass could think, or if the mayor was making that up. They seemed worried about the bass. They didn't look like they believed the mayor…

TINA ALMOST FELL out of her chair. She came when she imagined a largemouth, the one she'd touched as a child, the one she pinned beneath her hand as her father had explained how to remove the hook. She'd been afraid she wouldn't be able to keep it from thrashing on the floor of their aluminum boat, as her father said she must. *So you won't scare the others. So you won't hook yourself.* That's what Tina had feared, hooking herself. She couldn't imagine a worse thing. With her free hand, she'd grabbed the hook's shank—and pulled slowly, gently—tugging barb and point from the wet, white mouth, until it hung up on the thick, stubborn, cartilaginous lips and her father said *Rip it, Honey. Rip it out.*

TINA'S NAKED BREASTS BOUNCED when she rose to answer the phone she'd left in the kitchen. She stood in her tiger striped panties and curled her toes on the linoleum. *Hello?*

Hi, a man said. *I saw your little performance.*

What?

And I think you're pretty…

Who is this? Tina said. She looked out the kitchen window. She lived in a second-story apartment of a renovated farm house. She didn't understand how anyone could see into her living room, or see her in her chair. The south side window faced her neighbor's house, Frank Pulchaski's, and his dormer window was more or less opposite her living room, but no one other than the harmless old man lived there, and Tina's curtains were half drawn. Well, maybe if he had a visitor, and if the visitor were staying in that room, and had binoculars or a telescope…But she hadn't seen anyone over there lately, other than old Frank.

I'm a neighbor, the man said. *I'd like to come over.*

No!

Hey, take it easy.

I don't know you. I'm calling the police.

What will you tell them?

That a Peeping Tom is stalking me.

I'm not a peeper, he said.

What are you, then? What do you want?

See you in a minute, he said.

Tina threw on a shirt and climbed into her jeans. She could see whoever came up the stairs to her apartment. She could look through the window of the door, too, which she had covered with a shade. She could peek around the edges of the shade. The door was locked, so she was safe. The man could stand there on the porch at the top of the stairs and talk through the door. She could call 911 anytime. The cops could be there in two minutes.

She waited. She slipped the shade up. A squirrel like a tightrope walker crossed the power lines between her house and a distant pole. It was leaving with an apple slice she'd left on the birdfeeder, the feeder she'd placed on the porch railing. The squirrel teetered back and forth on its nimble legs. She hoped it wouldn't get electrocuted. It distracted her for a moment, then Tina put her nose close to the window and turned her head enough to see if anyone was climbing the stairs, which were built perpendicular to her apartment entrance and hugged the house's wall. Now she could see down to the bottom. She could see her mailbox. And then she saw a man beside it.

Tina pulled the shade down. She stepped back. *Had she turned the lock on the doorknob?* She thought she had. *Which way was it locked, with the doorknob doohickey vertical or horizontal?*

When he reached her doorway, his head and shoulders made a silhouette through the shade. She didn't have a doorbell, so he would have to knock. He didn't knock right away. He paused, and then he knocked. *Hello?* he said. He knocked again, lightly. *Hello?*

Who are you? Tina said.

Hey, hi! I'm Alex, your neighbor across the street, two houses down. Gray house, white trim?

Why did you call me?

Stacy and I saw you at the Snow Goose. Stacy Miller, Channel Six News. I'm her cameraman. We saw you serving Al Skillings, the Bass Master. He's always good for a negative sound bite about the tournaments. —That was quite a performance.

What are you talking about?

Talking him into apple pie. With Al, it's usually pecan or nothing at all.

Very observant, and creepy.

No. I saw you move in here, too, so I said to myself, hey...

Where else did you see me perform?

Nowhere. Should I have?

No, Tina said. She took a step forward and pulled on the shade. It snapped up quickly and startled them both.

Yow! Alex said. *I just thought...If you don't want to let me in, you can come over to my house sometime. When you feel like it. The gray one, number fifty-four...*

How did you get my number?

Angela at the diner. She'll tell me anything. Thinks I'm famous.

Why?

Why does she think I'm famous?

What do you want?

Well, I see you move in, I see you're cute. So I think,

*okay, she'll have about ten dates after working a week at
the Snow Goose, so I thought I'd try to beat the crowd. —
You're not going to open the door, are you.*

No.

*Okay. Guess I don't blame you. No hard feelings, I hope.
If you change your mind…* Alex went down the stairs.

Tina opened the door; peeked out. *Why does Angela
think you're famous?*

Alex stopped at the bottom. *I don't know. If you carry
a camera around, work for TV…*

You know Roman Buchholz?

Sure.

Come on up.

Seriously?

Yes, Tina said. *I just…you know, everyone has to be
careful, don't they?*

That's smart, Alex said. *You know Roman?* he asked,
climbing the stairs again.

Not really, she said. Tina let Alex through the door.
She reached out to shake his hand, but he kept his right
hand in his pocket. She offered him her left, then, and
he shook it.

I see him on the news, she said. *What's wrong with your
other hand?*

It's gone, he said. Alex pulled it from his pocket.
This is what I've got. He held up a prosthesis, with soft,
plastic fingers.

Wow, Tina said. *Are you a war vet?*

I'm a veteran logger, Alex said. *Forced retirement at twenty-five. I was holding up one end of a log that my partner was cutting through from the other side. He saw me, but he didn't see where my hand was.*

Ouch, Tina said. *Does it work?*

It works a bit. Awkwardly, but I can pick things up.

Pick that up. Tina pointed to a spoon beside her coffee cup.

You're kind of bossy, aren't you?

Well, you're kind of a brute. Scaring me, marching yourself over here.

Alex picked up the spoon. *Sugar?*

Ha, Tina said. She took the spoon from him. She put it down and grabbed his hand. It felt soft and supple, like a rubber toy frog. She followed it up to the elbow beneath his long sleeved shirt.

Yes, the forearm too, he said.

She led him into the living room. *I thought you were spying on me,* she said. *I thought you were a Peeping Tom.*

Not me, Alex said. *But you're directly across from Frank. Retired from the newspaper, fired from Channel Six. Have you met him?*

The day I moved in, Tina said. *He helped my father carry up the dryer. Asked if I liked the weather up here in Trout River.*

He was the solo weather man, Alex said. *Before they canned him....*

Really? A meteorologist?

Yes. That impress you? If it does, let me say that I wanted to be a weatherman, but they didn't want a plastic finger pointing to the map.

Alex dropped down on his knees for a better look out the window, peered across the space between Tina's and Frank's. He put his hand, his real one, on the window sill. *I see a lens,* he said. *Look. The window's open. Look through the shadows. See that shiny spot? That's a camera lens—or a telescope.*

You're kidding, Tina said.

Look, he said. *Someone is spying on you.*

Tina looked. *I don't know,* she said. She went to get her binoculars. She had a pretty good pair of eight-power Leupolds. She liked to watch birds. She liked to watch birds and squirrels. Sometimes she liked to look through the Leupolds backwards and make things tiny.

Shit, she said. As she looked through the binoculars, she thought she saw Frank move away from the window. *That old bastard.*

Well, now you know, Alex said.

Tina paced back and forth across the living room. She walked around a chair. *When you came in, you said I was cute. Didn't I hear you say that?*

You did. I think you're very cute.

Would you like to…fuck me? she said. Alex's eyes widened. Was that a shocking thing to say? Well, probably, but she meant it. She'd never been promiscuous outside of her fantasies with the television

and the weather men, but now she felt daring with
nothing to lose. *Put on a little show? Give the old guy…*

Are you serious?

Tina could see that he hoped she was. …*something to
remember*, she said. *Use your—you know, your hand.*

You're not serious.

No, really. Come on. Tina unzipped her jeans, pushed
them down to her knees.

You are serious, he said. *And you're very—direct.*

She showed Alex her tiger stripes. She stepped out of
her jeans and slipped off her panties. *Now you*, she said.

Now me what?

Use your imagination, she said. *You're famous.*

FRANK PULCHASKI WENT BACK to the window.
He thought he'd been seen, but he worked up enough
courage to go back. The show was always too good.
He hoped he'd been mistaken—that his new neighbor
had only appeared to be looking right at him—that
she really hadn't been. Occasionally he'd see her on
the porch early in the morning, looking through her
binoculars, aiming them at birds. He repositioned
himself, pulled the telescope on the tripod farther
back from the window, to reduce glare that could give
him away, that may have already given him away, and
refocused. And there she was: Naked Tina with her big
tits. But she was with that young man across the street,
that Alex Somebody. Who moved his entire arm back

and forth as if he were pumping a car jack, while Tina arched herself, legs spread, over the arm of her chair. She'd moved the chair closer to the window, it seemed to him, and held her hands up over her head, grabbing the back of the chair as if preparing to vault out of it. And through that open space, through a forty-five-power spotting scope, Tina's nipples, her soft pink areola, rose and fell into the black hole of Frank Pulchaski's eye.

Tina tilted her head. She arched her back and made a bridge of her body. Alex looked like he was trying to raise it, pumping his arm back and forth... Then Tina whimpered, her arching back collapsed, and she dropped out of the chair and onto the floor. Alex lifted her head up, cradled it like a pumpkin, and she unzipped him.

Stop! Frank yelled. He didn't want it to happen like this. This wasn't how it was supposed to go.

Tina looked over at Frank, twenty yards distant. *So, there you are. You like to watch? Watch this.*

He couldn't. He couldn't watch it. He got up and went to his closet. He found his old Remington hunting rifle—a .30-06 pump action with a six-shot clip—and shoved three bullets in the clip. Then he shoved the clip into the magazine and went back to the window.

Tina on her knees, slobber dripping from her chin, sucked Alex off.

Alex removed his prosthesis. He placed it in the chair. Tina stopped sucking to check it out. *Amazing,* she said. She placed it between her legs. *Okay?*

You can't hurt it, he said. *I'm the Terminator.*

I'm the Masturbator, she laughed. She groped for the middle finger.

Frank had never seen anything like it. His wife had never done things like that. She was dead now. She'd been shot by the woman who had lived in the apartment before Tina. That woman had walked into Frank's house when he wasn't home and shot his wife Mary, point blank, in the kitchen. Used a shotgun with buckshot. She'd thought Mary had stolen her baby, or something like that. The woman was crazy, had thrown her baby out the window—tried to kill it—but Mary went outside and picked it up. It had been alive when she'd tried to save it. Mary carried it back into the Pulchaski's own kitchen. She placed it in a blanket-lined cardboard box. The mother came in to take it back, and shot Mary in the face.

FRANK PUSHED HIS TELESCOPE ASIDE, rested the rifle barrel on the windowsill. Now he looked through the rifle's scope, a 3X–9X variable Burris, and at three power, put the crosshairs on Tina's temple. She'd finished and gotten up off her knees and sat on the edge of the chair. Alex's erection was softening and his hand was gone. Tina had it. Now she held it between her legs. With her other hand she held Alex's penis. She tried to pump and suck it back to life. *Again?* she said.

I don't know if I can. Of course you can. She paused for a moment and looked over toward Frank's. She couldn't see him, but she knew he was there.

Hey, Frank, she said, feeling cruel and exhilarated. *How's the view? Enjoying the weather?*

Frank eased off on the trigger and moved the crosshairs. He couldn't shoot Tina. Well he *could*— sometimes he really felt like it, but he didn't feel like it now. Now she was just being a bad girl. Tina was like a daughter to him—sometimes. Sometimes she was like the grown-up version of the baby his wife Mary had tried to rescue from that woman who used to live there. She *had* rescued it, and maybe it would've been theirs to keep if Mary hadn't been killed. The cops, when they arrived, removed the baby from the house. It hadn't been crying before, but after they picked it up, it started to bawl. One of them stayed with it in the cruiser. The other cop went back to wait for the detectives and the forensics crew. He almost shot Frank when he came home and entered the kitchen before anyone else had arrived.

I live here, Frank said. *That's my wife.*

TINA LOOKED OVER once more and realized that it was not a telescope resting on the window sill. *Oh, shit. This is…*

What? Alex said.

Frank shifted his aim and found Alex in the scope

and raised the power to nine. He placed the crosshairs on his erection coming back to life. *Hey, buddy,* he said. *Hey, pal.*

THE CLOSE-UP

ALEX SHIPLEY'S PENIS flew across the room. Frank Pulchaski, who'd lived next door, had shot it off with his .30-06. Four days later, Carla Rosen stood over the blood-stained carpet and imagined the horror, the young man looking down at his shredded genitals, unbelieving, as Frank—from his second story window, with a direct line of sight into the apartment's living room—shot him again, this time through the chest.

The cops said that Tina Kessler, the woman to whom Carla had rented the apartment, was sitting on the floor when they'd arrived. In shock, yet trying to talk between convulsive sobs, Tina finally, simply, pointed to the window. When they looked out, the cops saw Frank, who appeared to be sitting on a chair or a box, who sat smoking a cigar with the rifle cradled in his lap. They rushed over and took the gun away, handcuffed him, and walked him to the cruiser. One cop remained with Frank while the other went back to the apartment and escorted Tina out to a waiting ambulance. She was covered with blood, but it wasn't her own; it was her boyfriend's.

Later, Carla heard that Frank hadn't resisted; that he'd extinguished his cigar in an ashtray before the police had made it up the stairs, but he didn't offer any explanation for the carnage.

Now the young man was dead, Frank Pulchaski was in prison, and Tina Kessler had moved back to where she'd come from, someplace downstate near Oneonta.

THE WALL-TO-WALL CARPET had to go before Carla Rosen could rent the apartment again. It was the only other damage besides the bullet hole. One of the bullets had penetrated the wall. She thought a little spackle could take care of that. If Michael were still here, he'd fix it, but...he wasn't. She broke off small chips of drywall around the edges of the hole with her fingernail. Tomorrow she'd come back with the spackle and trowel. And Benny, her brother-in-law, said he'd help with the carpet. Together they could pull it out, cut it up, and stuff the pieces in the back of Benny's truck.

CARLA HAD ONCE LIVED in the apartment herself, before Michael bought the place, after he'd asked her to marry him. That was five years ago, before the trouble.

He'd sat in this very chair, this one she'd left behind
after moving out—a cardinal red upholstered armchair
with eagle talons carved at the base of its wooden legs,
gripping what looked like the top of a flagpole. Or
maybe it was a fish head. Michael had said they didn't
make them like that anymore.

That was the first evening she'd invited him over
for dinner. They'd met at a pizzeria where Michael
overheard Carla telling the take-out cashier how her
phone made a constant buzzing noise, which was why
she hadn't called in her order in advance. Michael said
Excuse me, but, I could fix that.

He came over and she cooked him a Cornish hen. It
took him one minute to repair her phone. He tightened
a loose wire where the line came into the house. They
had planned to go to a movie afterwards, but never
made it. They ate apple pie for dessert, drank wine,
and watched *Wheel of Fortune*. Michael guessed the
first phrase before she or the contestants did. It was a
song title. It was something by Marvin Gaye. *Your good
at this,* she said. At first they sat in chairs because she
didn't have a couch. After Michael guessed the song,
she got up from her chair—a less hideous one without
carved talons or scales or toes, but with ratty gray
upholstery—and went out to the kitchen for more wine.
Michael followed her out. *You're younger than me,* he'd
said. *I am?* she said. *How about that.*

Do people live below you? I thought I heard someone.

A married couple, Carla said. *Sometimes it's hard not to hear them.*

When they went back in the living room, they abandoned the chairs and sat on the floor. She changed the channel so she wouldn't have to look at the mummified beauty of Vanna White, and they watched something else. News, maybe. Carla couldn't remember that; she'd lost interest in TV when Michael began fiddling with the buttons on her blouse. After he managed to open them up, the clasp on her bra was next, and she reciprocated: unbuttoning, unzipping, and slipping out his penis. She hadn't wanted to put it in her mouth—not then—she wanted to use her hands and watch him come, and he didn't seem to mind that. Then he surprised her with a sudden and voluminous ejaculation, which made them both laugh like the children they were not.

Now, five years later, standing over the blood stains and beside the chair and looking out the window, she wondered if Frank Pulchaski had been watching them, but if she remembered correctly, the shades had been drawn, at least most of the way down. She had been careful about that and pulled them most of the way down, most of the time, and Frank's wife Mary was still living then, so maybe he'd been busy taking care of his sick wife—making her tea or propping her up with pillows so she could watch TV. Maybe he wasn't hanging out by the window with his telescope. Maybe

Frank was all right back then.

To think of Frank Pulchaski watching while Michael came all over her. Did he get a close-up view of that?— She hoped not. It was too gross to imagine.

But now Frank was gone and her husband was dead. She tried not to feel sorry for herself. That was easy to do, to dwell on your bad luck and feel cheated out of something. But she *had* been cheated out of something: her husband. Michael had died suddenly at the age of forty-six. Everybody knew that was too soon; he was still young. Her friends and family had repeatedly expressed and reinforced those notions in their condolences and disbelief, but it did little to relieve Carla's grief, which, for a year, maybe two, spread like a fungal blight in the garden of normalcy, laughter, and peace—bringing her to tears suddenly and at odd moments—until, without fanfare, it died, and left her with a sadness more manageable for what remained and for what Michael had given.

TELL THE TENANTS *to do their own shoveling or hire their own plow guy*, she'd said, but no, Michael had said he'd rather take care of it, as he'd taken care of the lawn—so he plowed out the driveway with his pickup, shoveled their pathways, and salted their steps. One evening after a February storm he'd come home to their new residence, a slate-roofed Colonial with its own yard and crab apple, and, after eating dinner said, *I don't feel so good.* And Carla remembered saying, *Why should you expect to? After doing all that.*

They'd sat together and watched the news. Carla drank Coke and nibbled Orville Redenbacher's microwave buttered popcorn. Michael passed on the popcorn. He sipped a Coke. Then he fell off the couch, upending the popcorn bowl and spilling his soda, and vomited on the new rug she'd bought from L.L. Bean, a blue-braided circular one they'd placed beneath the coffee table. She called 911 and tried to revive him. Popcorn kernels floated in the vomit; she crunched a couple beneath her knees. She put the phone on speaker mode so she could listen to instructions and use both hands to compress his chest, but—*How much pressure? How many times?* The EMT's when they got there couldn't revive him either. They rushed him to the ER and everyone kept trying to save him, until a nurse came through a swinging door and said she was sorry, followed by a very black doctor who said he was sorry too. He touched her on the shoulder. His eyes, in that black face, were startlingly white, bordering deep brown pools of sympathy, regret, and—was it impotence? Is that what she saw? That rare thing, that non-admission, in a man, and, she had thought, that nonexistent thing in a doctor—in a cardiologist. Carla nodded *thank you*; she couldn't speak through tears, then she prayed he'd go away before Michael's racist father arrived to complicate an already impossible day.

*

TWO YEARS BEFORE MICHAEL DIED, he'd bought the house Carla had lived in—an old two-story farmhouse that had been converted into two apartments, one upstairs and one down—with lath and plaster walls and striped wallpaper covered over by dark wood paneling, and the faint but undeniable odor of mice and vermin.

Her husband bought a couple of other fixer-uppers too, leaving her with more property and stranding her with the headaches of ownership; but Michael's sister had married handyman Benjamin Swank, so he helped with most of the problems that seemed to occur almost weekly at one place or another. While Benny took care of the hassles, Carla collected the rent.

Michael had been right. *People will live anywhere. They will live anywhere and pay almost anything you ask them to pay because the next landlord down the block will ask them to pay even more for a worse dump than the one you're showing them.* Carla didn't know that's how it worked until Michael had said that and shown her the numbers.

"See? Look. That's why I'm buying the house you lived in. We'll paint it, put in a new toilet, lay new linoleum in the kitchen, and then we'll rent it, sit back, and live on easy street."

Michael had been a lineman for the phone company, and he ran his own electrical and plumbing business on the side. He'd counted on his brother-in-law to help him out with the apartments, if he'd needed it, as Carla counted on him now. Weekdays, Benny Swank worked regular hours as a boiler maintenance technician at the local college.

CARLA WONDERED NOW what would happen to Frank Pulchaski's house. It was up for sale. It wasn't in bad condition. The Polish knew how to take care of things. They didn't want anyone to think there was something they couldn't fix. They didn't want anyone to think they weren't perfectly, competently Catholic. Carla was Catholic too, but it was hard, she thought, to be as Catholic as the Polish.

Frank's wife, Mary Pulchaski, used to hang flags from a pole off their front porch. Carla called them *happy flags*. She didn't know what Mary called them. They were colorful flags depicting flowers, or simple, stylized renderings of dogs or birds. On important days, Mary flew the American flag instead of a happy flag. Carla believed that Frank was a veteran of some war because of that, and because he often wore a camouflage cap, but other times she thought maybe he was just a hunter because he drove a Ford pickup and wore a red-and-black checkered jacket, although she never saw him with a gun or a deer in the back of his truck.

IN THE APARTMENT, Carla now sat in the red chair with bird claws and looked at the blood. It ran in

crazy spiraled ribbons across the floor. It lay in lumpy
pools, like spilled paint. It speckled the carpet black.
The blood made it hard to think about anything nice.
Absentmindedly she ran her fingers through her hair,
down her neck and to her chest, and touched the
place where Michael had dribbled so much of himself
between her breasts, the breasts she may have shared
with Frank Pulchaski.

*

WHEN CARLA LEFT the apartment, she used the back
staircase that all the tenants, including Tina Kessler,
had used as their main entrance. The railing wobbled in
her hand. She worried about liability, about someone
taking a tumble down the stairs. She would talk to
Benny about replacing some of those punky steps with
pressure treated wood; she'd ask him what he thought
about the railing. She had insurance, but a small
investment was worth it if it kept you living on easy
street.

   Before going home, Carla thought she'd take a
peek inside the Pulchaski house. Since a *For Sale*
sign had appeared on the front porch, she'd seen a
cleaning crew coming and going the last few days
with their equipment, and she was curious to see how
things looked. She crossed the driveway between
her apartment house and the Pulchaskis, and tried
looking through the entryway window to the kitchen

when she got there. But it was hard to see beyond the windowpane's reflection of her own curious face.

She tried the screen door and found it unlocked. When she opened it, the wooden door behind it swung open on its own. It wasn't locked either. It opened itself. She knocked on the doorframe. *Hello? Anyone here?* She thought it wouldn't hurt to step inside.

The place had been purged of the Pulchaskis. The cupboard doors remained open, with a box of D-con in each cupboard. The linoleum floor, clean and shiny, had been recently washed and waxed.

Carla walked through the kitchen, then into the dining room and then the living room. She looked through the front windows out onto the porch—no happy flag—and into the street. Then moving upstairs, she ran her fingers over the textured wallpaper of a narrow hallway. She came to the door of the room where Frank had spied on Tina Kessler and shot Alex Shipley. She stood outside for a moment. When she entered, she was surprised to find a telescope perched on a tripod's straddled legs.

Someone had placed a chair behind the scope—a chair whose antique-white finish Carla admired, along with its curved and arched back rail and bentwood braces. On the floor, a candy wrapper, an empty can of Coke. A roll of duct tape.

"Hi."

"Yikes!" Carla pivoted quickly; she almost lost her

balance. "Who are you? You scared the shit out of me."

"Jefferson Page. Century 21. Interested?" Jefferson Page stood in the doorway. Then he entered the room and held out a hand—pale and long-fingered, well-manicured and clean. She shook it. It felt soft and warm, like a newborn squirrel she had to be careful not to squeeze.

"Imagine that old bastard, huh?" He pulled his hand away and sat down behind the telescope. "This is mine," he admitted. "Twenty-to-sixty power variable Zeiss. Top of the line. Well, almost. It's not a Swarovski. I brought it up here to see what it must've been like."

"To see what *what* must've been like?"

"No! No. Oh, I suppose it looks bad," he said. "But no. To imagine what the old guy was thinking. You know, his *mindset*, and what he saw that made him—"

"—shoot that young man's penis off, then kill him?"

"Yes, I know. Horrible."

"In my apartment," Carla said. "With my tenant."

"I'm sorry," Jefferson Page said. He looked through the scope and focused the eyepiece. "I saw you earlier, too—over there."

"You were watching me?"

"I didn't mean to. I didn't expect anyone to be in the apartment. They're not, are they? I mean, you don't have a new tenant yet, do you? And downstairs…"

"Everyone moved out after the shooting. You're changing the subject."

"I apologize. Please. If you insist on being angry, I'll have to say that you're trespassing."

Carla flushed. "I was just…"

"Can we call it even?" Jefferson Page stood up.

"Well, you haven't really explained all this." Carla pointed to the scope, the trash on the floor.

"I told you. Why did he do it? I thought, if I sat here for a bit…I thought the apartment was vacant. I normally use the scope for hunting. Sometimes I travel out west, hunt elk in the mountains…" he paused and then he stopped. "I don't know what else to say."

"You snuck up on me," Carla said. "You're a peeper."

"No," he said. "I'm a realtor. I was waiting to meet a client. I thought you were the guy. Here's my card. Call my boss, Jason Beggs. Check me out."

Carla took Jefferson Page's card. It had a picture of him on it, wearing the same shirt he wore now: a black polo with white monogramming over the pocket. The card itself was yellow with green print. It made her think of St. Patrick's Day, of Notre Dame football and the Fighting Irish. "You have an old-fashioned name," she said.

"Yeah," he said. "My family's out of Mississippi. That's Jefferson as in Jefferson Davis, not Thomas."

"Oh," Carla said. She didn't know what that meant.

"Hey, the war's over, isn't it? My father says you look back far enough, we all came out of the swamp. Sometimes he'd say…well, I can't say what he said. I don't know. How about I go over to the apartment and you stay here. Then take a look yourself through the telescope, and we'll call it even. Okay?"

Carla shrugged her shoulders. *The swamp? What war was he talking about?* "I knocked before I entered," she said. "I called out. You must have heard me."

"No," he said. "I didn't." Jefferson Page bolted out of the room, down the stairs, and across the lot.

What would he do over there, in her apartment? Probably wanted an excuse to see how much blood Alex Shipley had spilled, or to slip his finger in the bullet hole in the wall.

Carla sat in the chair, again admiring the craftsmanship in the subtle curvature of the seat, and put her eye to the eyepiece after telling herself she would not. The shade on the Pulchaski's window had been removed, and the shade on her apartment window was drawn all the way up. Then Jefferson Page appeared. Carla pulled her eye away from the scope. She looked down at the floor, at the Coke can and the candy wrapper; the duct tape was gone. She looked back up and out. Jefferson Page waved and opened the window.

He mimed with his hands: *Up, up.* He wanted her to raise the window, but she didn't see why she should. The glass was clean; the view was good. Then she heard him say: "Go on, raise it."

They were about twenty yards apart. Carla held her hands palms up: *why?*

"So I don't have to shout," he shouted.

Carla unlatched the lock. She raised the window.

"Jesus Christ," he said. "You've got quite a mess here." When she didn't respond, he continued: "So, the guy wasn't even her boyfriend? Is that right?"

"I don't know if anyone knows for sure," she said.

"I heard it was his first time over. How old? Twenty-four? Something like that, right? I heard she was, what—on her knees?—when Pulchaski let him have it. How come he didn't shoot her? I mean, why the *guy*? Jesus Christ, two people, and then…You're going to need a new carpet. This looks like a slaughter house."

"Are you finished now? Why don't you come back."

"In a minute. —Did I see you take a peek through the telescope?"

"Yes. Yes I did."

"What did you see?"

"What?"

"What did you see?"

"Nothing. There was nothing."

"Nothing?"

"No."

"But you saw me, didn't you?"

"I suppose I did, for a second."

"Magnified."

"Yes, but I can see you just fine without looking through it."

"It's not the same though. Look again. If you look

through the scope, part of me will be magnified times sixty. Go on."

"No thanks."

"You're not interested in the close-up? The zoom-in?"

"I don't think so," she said.

"Interesting. Most people, they want to be the fly on the wall. They want to penetrate other people's lives. *Be there*, get inside. Climb into their underpants."

"Not me," Carla said.

THEN JEFFERSON PAGE WAS GONE from sight. He was probably snooping around, checking out the blood stains or looking for the bullet hole. Frank Pulchaski had fired twice, but there was only one exit wound from the first shot and one hole in the wall. The second bullet had lodged itself in Alex Shipley's spine after shattering the sternum and passing through the heart.

Carla reexamined Jefferson Page's business card. He looked like a realtor in that polo shirt; he looked like a guy who'd sell you a house with termites. She studied the clover green print and wondered if he was a college football fan. She wondered if she could do business with a man who hunted elk. When she was thinking of what it would be like to shoot such a majestic animal, Jefferson Page reappeared in the apartment window, but not suddenly out of nowhere, like a snake or a deer, as he had when they had first met. Now he shuffled and stutter-stepped. She didn't need the scope to see that his head was wrapped in duct tape. A gap below his nostrils between the strips of tape allowed him to breathe, but the tape covered the bridge of his nose and most of his face. A tuft of brown hair, like paintbrush bristles, rose up on top of his head. And Jefferson Page was naked.

It took Carla a moment to realize that he wasn't a victim of some horrible act, but the actor. He stood with a hand reaching out dramatically for the edges of the window frame and, with the other, fondling himself.

Carla's first impulse was to leap out of the chair and flee the Pulchaski house, get to her car and drive away, but she didn't. Instead she put her eye to the telescope, where the head of Jefferson's penis rose like an emergent spring bulb. It filled up the entire lens. He'd said it was a variable scope—that meant you could change it—so she twisted the eyepiece from 60X to 20X and, sure enough, reduced the magnification, yet what she saw remained immense and imploring, and she could not make herself look away.

Jefferson Page had nice hands, as she'd noticed earlier, with long, well-manicured fingers. Now she watched them encircle his shaft to stroke, pull, and titillate as a glistening sheen of mucous mysteriously appeared— saliva spittle dropped from lips disembodied from the circle of her perception. She felt her heartbeat like a strumming and watched Jefferson's fingers slip down to his balls, giving her another view of his erection—*times twenty*—and Carla, shifting her weight on the expertly crafted reproduction of an early 20th century chair, slid forward and back on the hard maple seat, on pickled white paint, her body electrified by Jefferson Page— duct-taped blind, deaf and dumb, from Century 21— who, in a moment of sublime perversion and release, let semen burst forth like fluttering doves from a hat.

"Oh," Carla said, flushed and a bit unhinged, lost in a moment of pleasure, shuddering shamefully. And yet where was the shame when you were not the uninvited guest, but the privileged invitee? No, actually, she knew. Through the eye of a needle, through the eye of a telescope. *Into the swamp.* To be breathlessly engulfed by the zoom-in. Now she followed what had been her first impulse. She hoped she could be gone by the time Jefferson unwrapped his head and got dressed. She scuttled out of the bedroom, tripped down the stairs, and skidded and fell on the kitchen's freshly waxed floor. She landed on her ass, got back on her feet, and scrambled out the door and to her car parked in back of the apartment. She got in and started backing out. From her place behind the wheel and the car's proximity to the house, Carla couldn't see up into the window where Jefferson was. When she had backed out into the road, he reappeared to her again, emerging shirtless from the back stairway; he tripped on the bottom step. He walked toward her over lawn grass in need of mowing. His polo shirt, sandwiched between an elbow and his ribs, looked for a moment like a little black dog. The shirt's collar flapped like floppy ears while Jefferson used both hands to buckle his belt.

"Hey!" he said. "Enjoy the show?"

"I don't think—not as much as you," she said.

"Well, it's what you get for free admission." He slipped his shirt on. "I left my shoes and socks upstairs, and I think I caught a splinter on your steps."

"You duct taped your head."

"Yes, the zombie effect. Whatever it takes." Balanced on one leg like a stork, he craned his neck and peered at his foot.

"And the zombie came on my carpet," Carla said.

"That's hardly the worst of it, is it?" he said. "Hey, you got a needle on you?"

"No. See you later, Jefferson Page."

"Wait! Wait. About that carpet. Could I dispose of it? Could I take it? I'll have it out by day's end."

"You want the blood-stained carpet."

"If you wouldn't mind."

Carla thought of all the work that would save her and her brother-in-law Benny. "Why?"

"I'm interested," he said.

She laughed.

"I'm not kidding," he said.

"Okay, I guess. Why not? Pull up the carpet tacks too while you're at it." Then she thought about it and said, "And the chair. Take that too, we'll call it even."

"The red one, with the bird feet?"

"Yes," she said. "I'd like to get rid of that as well."
Carla looked at Jefferson's hands. They didn't look
so good to her now: one holding his foot, the other
impotently groping for the splinter with pale white
fingers. It seemed as though she hadn't noticed before all
the dark hair on his knuckles. How could she have not?

"You help me out here, we've got a deal," he said.

"The carpet *and* the chair?" she said.

"I'll take them both. Come on now. Play nurse."

Carla got out of the car, closed the door behind her,
and then dropped to her knees behind Jefferson Page.
She cradled his upturned foot in her left hand, and with
her free hand tried to grasp the splinter. It was visible,
but barely protruding where it had broken off in the soft
curl of his arch. It was black and slick with blood; she
would think she had it and give it a tug, only to have it
slip away. "It's deep," she said. "Does it hurt?"

"A little bit."

"It's hard to grasp."

"When you touch it, I feel it move inside me."

"Be still," she said.

Jefferson looked down at the top of Carla's head.
He twisted his neck and torso so he could look behind
himself and watch. He trusted her. He looked down the
front of her blouse. "If people could see us now…" he
said.

"I hope no one does."

"The way you're holding…"

"THERE!" SHE SAID. "Got it. You might want Neosporin when you get home."

"Thank you. It feels…Wow, that's a monster, huh? They say you pierce a body two inches deep, it's a potentially fatal wound."

"I think you've got at least an inch of grace," she said.

"I hope so," he said. "But you're passing on the close-up, am I right?"

"The close-up?" She looked at the splinter cradled in the palm of her hand. She thought of Frank Pulchaski peeping out his window. When had he begun to do that? What had he seen? She remembered pulling the shades down most of the way, most of the time. If she hadn't pulled them completely down, did a three-or-four-inch gap between the sill and the shade allow enough space for a telescopic eye to enter? Had Frank repeatedly witnessed the breathless intimacy of their love making? Had her nipples been magnified times sixty?

The splinter she'd plucked from Jefferson's foot looked long and sharp and nasty. It was curved like a claw. Forgetting herself for a moment, she stood and held it out to him. "Here," she said. "The close-up? Call it whatever you want, but whatever you call it, take it with you. And thanks. Thanks for taking the chair."

ACKNOWLEDGMENTS

"The New Baby" was first published by *Indiana Review* in 2010.

COLOPHON

Text is set in a digital version of Jenson, designed by
Robert Slimbach in 1996, and based on the work of
punchcutter, printer, and publisher Nicolas Jenson.

The titles are set in Futura.

MARK HOLDEN teaches creative writing at Plattsburgh State University in New York. He received the Lamar York nonfiction award from *Chattahoochee Review* and the Kurt Vonnegut fiction award from *North American Review* in 2005. His work has also appeared in *Georgia Review, Bellevue Review, New Millennium Writings*, and others.

NEW MICHIGAN PRESS, based in Tucson, Arizona, prints poetry and prose chapbooks, especially work that transcends traditional genre. Together with DIAGRAM, NMP sponsors a yearly chapbook competition.

DIAGRAM, a journal of text, art, and schematic, is published bimonthly at THEDIAGRAM.COM. Periodic print anthologies are available from the New Michigan Press at NEWMICHIGANPRESS.COM/NMP.